Nursery Rhymes
Wee Willie Winkie
and Other Best-loved Rhymes

alphabet
soup

an imprint of

WINDMILL
BOOKS
New York

Published in 2009 by Windmill Books, LLC
303 Park Avenue South, Suite # 1280, New York, NY 10010-3657

Illustrations by Ulkutay & Co. Ltd.
Editor: Rebecca Gerlings
Compiler: Paige Weber

      Publisher Cataloging Data

Wee Willie Winkie and other best-loved rhymes / edited by Rebecca Gerlings.
p.   cm. – (Nursery rhymes)
Contents: Wee Willie Winkie—Little Bo Peep—There was an old woman who lived in a shoe—
Red sky at morning—I saw a ship a-sailing—The little robin—Simple Simon—
Hickory, dickory, dock!—Eenie, meenie, minie, Moe—If all the world.
ISBN 978-1-60754-137-0 (library binding)
ISBN 978-1-60754-138-7 (paperback)
ISBN 978-1-60754-139-4 (6-pack)
1. Nursery rhymes 2. Children's poetry [1. Nursery rhymes]
I. Gerlings, Rebecca II. Mother Goose III. Series
          398.8—dc22

Printed in the United States

For more great fiction and nonfiction, go to windmillbks.com.

CONTENTS

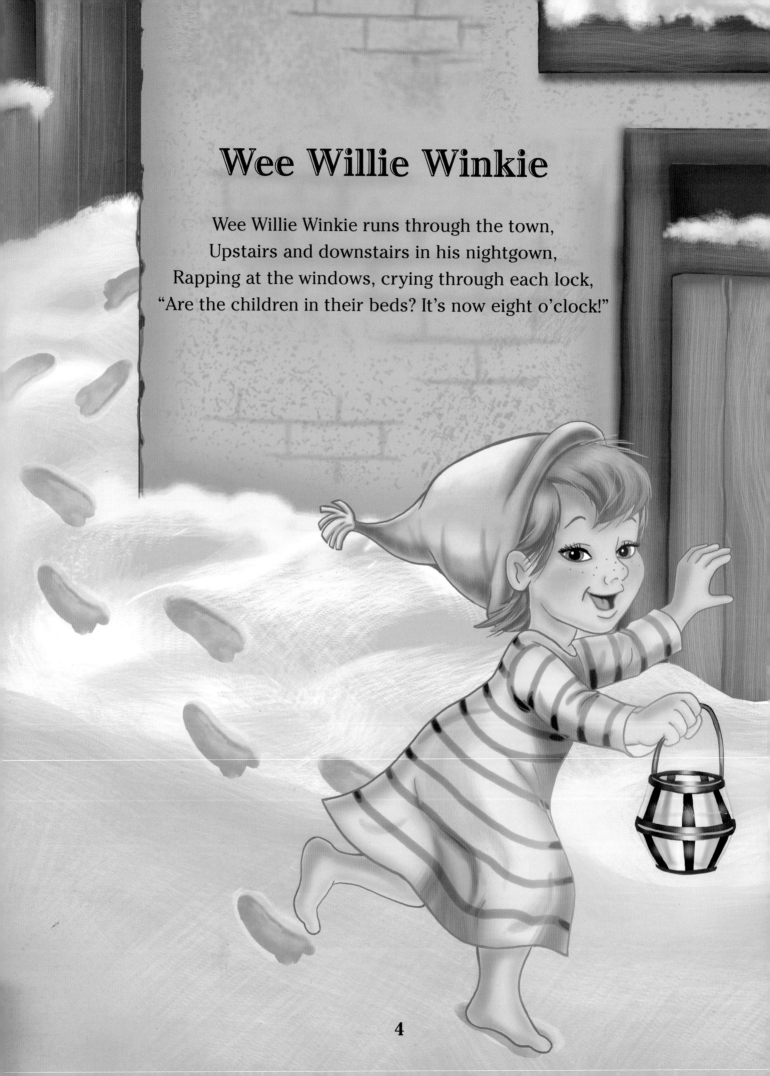

Wee Willie Winkie

Wee Willie Winkie runs through the town,
Upstairs and downstairs in his nightgown,
Rapping at the windows, crying through each lock,
"Are the children in their beds? It's now eight o'clock!"

Little Bo Peep

Little Bo Peep has lost her sheep,
And can't tell where to find them.
Leave them alone, and they'll come home,
Wagging their tails behind them.

Little Bo Peep fell fast asleep
And dreamed she heard them bleating.
But when she awoke she found it a joke,
For they were still all fleeting.

Then up she took her little crook,
Determined for to find them.
She found them indeed, but it made her heart bleed,
For they'd left their tails behind them.

It happened one day, as Bo Peep did stray
Over a meadow hard by,
That there she espied their tails, side by side,
All hung on a tree to dry.

She heaved a sigh and wiped her eye,
Then over the hills she raced
And tried what she could, as a shepherdess should,
So each tail would be properly placed.

There Was an Old Woman Who Lived In a Shoe

There was an old woman
Who lived in a shoe.
She had so many children
She didn't know what to do.
She gave them some broth,
Without any bread,
Then kissed them all quickly
And sent them to bed.

Red Sky at Morning

Red sky at morning,
Sailors take warning.
Red sky at night,
Sailor's delight.

I Saw A Ship A-Sailing

I saw a ship a-sailing,
A-sailing on the sea.
And, oh, it was all laden,
With pretty things for thee!

There were candies in the cabin,
And apples in the hold.
The sails were made of silk,
And the masts were made of gold.

The four and twenty sailors
That stood between the decks
Were four and twenty mice
With gold chains about their necks.

The captain was a duck
With a packet on his back.
And when the ship began to move,
The captain said, "Quack! Quack!"

The Little Robin

The little robin grieves
When the snow is on the ground,
For the trees have no leaves
And no berries can be found.

The air is cold, the worms are hid.
For robin here, what can be done?
Let's throw around some crumbs of bread,
And then he'll live till snow is gone.

Simple Simon

Simple Simon met a pieman
Going to the fair.
Simple Simon asked the pieman,
"Let me taste your ware."

Said the pieman to Simple Simon,
"Show me first your penny."
Simple Simon told the pieman,
"Indeed I have not any."

Simple Simon went out fishing
For to catch a whale.
All the water he had got
Was in his mother's pail!

Simple Simon went to see
If plums grew on a thistle.
He pricked his finger very much,
Which made poor Simon whistle.

He went to catch a dickey bird,
And thought he could not fail,
Because he'd found a little salt
To put upon its tail.

He went for water with a sieve,
But soon it all ran through.
And now poor Simple Simon
Bids you a fond adieu.

Hickory, Dickory, Dock!

Hickory, dickory, dock!
The mouse ran up the clock.
The clock struck one,
The mouse ran down.
Hickory, dickory, dock!

Eenie, Meenie, Minie, Moe

Eenie, Meenie, Minie, Moe,
Catch a tiger by the toe.
If he hollers, let him go,
Eenie, Meenie, Minie, Moe.

25

If All The World

If all the world were apple pie,
And all the sea were ink,
And all the trees were bread and cheese,
What should we have for drink?

ABOUT THE RHYMES

Many people learned nursery rhymes when they were children, but not many know that these endearing little poems may be several centuries old. Nursery rhymes have endured through generations, sometimes carrying strange details from past ways of life. And some nursery rhymes are more than just playful children's verses. In fact, many reflect important historical events.

The rhymes' lyrics were often used to mock political events of their day, in times when any direct challenge of the establishment might carry serious consequences. But authors could conceal their messages in these seemingly innocent children's verses, and only certain people would understand. As a result, nursery rhymes constitute a valuable link between present and past.

Because the rhymes were often passed down orally, myriad interpretations exist. The following are some popular interpretations of the rhymes included in this book. If you are curious about the origins of other rhymes, see what you can find out on your own! Each one is rich with history.

Wee Willie Winkie

Penned at a time when the town crier was a prominent member of society and a very useful source of information, the character Wee Willie Winkie is a small boy turned town crier. Written by the Scottish poet William Miller, this short rhyme was first published in 1841. During the course of the tale, Wee Willie Winkie runs through the town alerting people to the fact that it is eight o'clock and all the children should be in bed. Today, most children can relate to the rhyme because they still experience bedtime routines.

Little Bo Peep

The name of the shepherdess in this nursery rhyme comes from the words that *bleat* and *sheep* are derived from. This moralistic tale cannot be directly traced to a historic occurrence. The message behind this tale is that you shouldn't fall short of your responsibilities, or you will have to pay the price. Little Bo Peep awakes from a slumber to find her sheep have disappeared and that their tails are hanging on a tree. The rhyme ends with her trying to somehow put the tails back on the sheep.

There Was an Old Woman Who Lived In a Shoe

There are different opinions as to the origins of this rhyme. The old woman in question, who had so many children she didn't know what to do, may have been Queen Caroline, who was married to the British king George II and had eight offspring. Alternatively, rather than representing an actual woman, the old woman may have been a man who people said was acting like an old woman, as in the case of King George and his white wigs. In this interpretation, the many children in the shoe are a reference to the members of parliament.

Simple Simon

Street sellers, such as the pieman who is mentioned at the start of "Simple Simon," were a common sight in old England. From medieval times onward, such early entrepreneurs often sold their goods at fairs, such as the one referred to in the rhyme. "Simple Simon" is also an example of how the word *adieu* was written into nursery rhymes instead of the word *goodbye*. The children's game Simon Says, in which children have to repeat the actions of a child playing the role of Simon, is also based on the character in this nursery rhyme.

Hickory, Dickory, Dock!

This well-known nursery rhyme encourages children to mimic the sound of a clock chiming and introduces them to the concept of telling time. The first publication date for this rhyme is 1744 and investigation into its origin has led people to believe that it has its roots in America. *Hickory* is a word derived from the North American Indian word *pawcohiccora* – a kind of milk or oily liquor pressed from pounded hickory nuts from the hickory tree. Dock is a species of plant that can be used medicinally as an astringent and tonic. You might need the soothing properties of the dock leaf after you are stung by a nettle!